She of the Rib
Women Unwrapped

Other Books of Poems
by Jayne Jaudon Ferrer

A New Mother's Prayers

A Mother of Sons

Dancing with My Daughter

She of the Rib
Women Unwrapped

Jayne Jaudon Ferrer

CRM BOOKS
Publishing Hope for Today's Society
Inspirational Books~CDs~Children's Books

Cover design: John Letterle

"Screen Test" and "Uteropian Myth" were first
published in the August 2004 issue of *Long Story
Short*. "Ex-Terminator" was first published in the
October 2005 issue of *Western North Carolina
Woman*.

CRM BOOKS
P.O. Box 2124
Hendersonville, NC 28793
www.ciridmus.com

Printed in the United States of America

ISBN: 1-933341-05-X
LCCN: 200695445

For Carlynne, Cheryl, and Kristy—
who have—literally!—always been there.

Contents

Acknowledgments

*W*omen's time on earth is spent in a diversity of roles: daughter, sister, mother, grandmother, aunt, niece, cousin, friend, lover, spouse, teacher, student, and on and on. There are as many different roles for us to play as there are variations on our shapes and appearance.

We may differ from role to role; indeed, we may differ within the *same* role, depending on our interactions with others. And that is the beauty of woman: that we are ever-changing, ever-growing, ever-discovering a new persona. Each day brings the chance to "unwrap," if you will, a new layer of ourselves.

I have known many marvelous women in my life.

Some I cherish for their love and support, some for their achievements and effort, some for their attitude and outlook. Lola Dietz taught me to love books when I was barely old enough to hold one; Ruby Miller taught me patience and pride and how to make great beef stew; my Aunt Burma, Aunt Erma, Aunt Mildred, Aunt Mozelle, Aunt Virginia, Aunt Woodie, Aunt Lois, and Aunt Eula taught me, respectively, the importance of peacefulness, playfulness, beauty, duty, independence, whimsy, kindness, and gumption; Dot Nichols and Caroline Doub have taught me how to age gracefully and with humor; my mother taught me that the only barrier to accomplishing any task is myself; my sister has taught me to focus on what truly matters; and a dozen different teachers and friends along the way have taught me, from their own unique perspective, that you really do get out of life exactly what you put into it.

It is through these women I have known—and through women I read about, or meet briefly, or hear speak, or admire from afar—that I have become the woman *I* am. I hope, through the reading of words distilled from their lessons to me, you discover the woman *you* have the good fortune to be.

Blessings,
Jayne Jaudon Ferrer

Life

Road Trip

At fifty, my faith is faltering.
Even as I pray "Thy will be done,"
I find myself wanting answers.
Why *do* bad things happen to good people?
Why do bad people get away with murder?
And what about liberty and justice for all?
True, we were never promised peace on earth;
And God never said life would be simple—
just that He'd be along for the ride.
A comfort, that—but scoot over, Padre.
I need to improve my grip.

Future Shock

Sometimes at night when there is only me,
I remember
a teacher's pet who always knew the answers,
a coy coquette who danced and laughed till dawn,
a corner office with leather and chrome and plaques.
Then the baby cries and I am back.
A wife
A mother
A woman who took the road less traveled.
And, indeed, that has made all the difference.

Street Scene

I think, at first, she is laughing.
No, drunk. Or high, or crazy, perhaps.
She circles on the broken sidewalk,
fumbling with her bags, stumbling from the weight.
At the red light, I watch, in judgment.
Low life. Trash. Delusional loser.
And then I see her tears, her face—
a wretched bas relief of anguish,
and my heart goes soft with new perspective.
In an instant I know this is a woman abandoned.
Her self-esteem shattered, her self-control consumed,
she is here with her every possession on display,
dumped like discarded ballast.

She staggers, lost, weeping north, and then west.
South; again, west.
I am staggered as well.
Could my life be so succinctly shoved
into a trio of bags?
Could my place in the world be so suddenly slashed
to a slice of sidewalk?
I decide, at last, to console her.
But when I circle the block,
she is gone.

Epiphany at St. Simons

Three impassioned middle-aged blondes
AWOL in a Georgia night—
brains on fire,
blood pumped up,
bravura at pinnacle height.
On a lighthouse bridge, they stand
watching barge and boat shadows ribbon past—
spirits soaring,
souls unleashed,
unfettered and free at last.

As grey waves surge, crest white,
then lurch and burble on the shore,
they vow to accomplish fresh goals and dreams
fueled by esprit de corps.
Emancipated, intrepid blondes,
inspired by a coastal moon,
go home, get busy. . .
they'll get to their dreams. . .
not today, of course,
but soon.

For Better, For Worse

Like a fork ripping cold steel tines down
the smooth jade flesh of a summer cucumber,
his piercing, slurred invectives rake her dignity
once again.

"Naggin' ol' woman. . .always naggin' 'bout this,
naggin' 'bout that. Why'd I marry you anyway?"
A belch. A wheeze. A cackle. A cough.

"You're a mean ol' woman, you know that?
A mean, ugly, naggin' ol' woman."
Another swig. Sweet silence, short-lived.

"Well, I ain't listenin' to you, do you hear?
I ain't doin' a blessed thing you say!

Her ears don't hear the last.
The water from the faucet's too loud in the sink
where, yet again, she stands rinsing
the stench and soil from her once crisp and white,
now limp and dingy, sheets.

Only her heart hears as she slumps, in tears—
ravaged dreams sliding down the drain with the
filthy, hate-stained suds.

The Ex-Terminator

I know
that every time I am lazy
and leave dishes in the sink until morning
those virulent roaches call the hot line and have a
house party.
But life is like that, I guess.
Let things slide while you take a
        quickbreath
and before you know it,
people are crawling all over you—
needing this, wanting that,
advising this, demanding that.
What *I* need is a giant can of Raid
to get everyone off my back
and back into their drainpipes.

Screen Test

She doesn't know she's beautiful,
has no idea her gaunt cheeks
haunting eyes
waifish body
and tousled hair
would be worth three thousand a day
on a runway in Paris.
Has no idea
that if the camera lens
now zooming in to capture
every blink of her black velvet eye
every tremble of her delicate chin
every tilt of her fine-boned head
belonged to Miramax
instead of CNN,
the director's slate would snap
and this hell would fade to black—
just a scene,
and a badly spliced memory.

To Whom It May Concern

Dear Cretin,
This is to let you know
you are a first-class, feeble-brained
jerk.
On what planet did you think it would be
okay to sleep with your wife's best friend?
Spare me your tale of woe, you louse.
I *know* what your home life was like.
You were loved and respected,
encouraged and helped
by a woman whose smile is now
missing,
by a daughter whose heart is now
crushed,
by a son who no longer wants to be
just like Dad.

In fact, what he wants to be
is dead, because you have
destroyed his world and his
faith and his trust,
all for a change of scenery.
You are the one who should
die, you cad.
Slowly,
roasted naked over a rotating
spit, your nether regions giving
"hottie" a whole new meaning.
She'll survive, you know—even thrive
(although your children may be damaged for life).
Because a good woman—
a smart, strong, fine and faithful woman—
needs a bad man like the Titanic
needed ice.

Observations on the Eve of My Fortieth Birthday

On the one hand, it seems a very long time
since Susie Knox and I chased grasshoppers in
Mother's marigolds, Dixie cups and crinolines
bouncing in the breeze.
On the other hand, it seems mere days ago
that Susie swept into our tenth reunion,
regal in royal blue, light years removed
from the Quickdraw McGraw sketches she parlayed
into a career in interior design.
Strange. I can't remember the names of guys
I thought I was in love with in college,
yet I recall every scene of the day in first grade
when Mark Hayman laughed after I got a spanking.
(*He* got one, then—the only redeeming thing
that wretched teacher ever did!)

All those afternoons sipping cherry Cokes
in Beeson's Drug Store. . .
all those evenings circling Knight's drive-in
and dragging Main. . .
how can that have happened *twenty-five years* ago?
Remember how unbelievable it was
when we used to hear grown-ups talk about
life before color TV and central air?
How stupid we thought they were
because they didn't know Paul from John and
because they hated Jimi Hendrix?
So talk about 8-track tape players and Nehru jackets
and see if teen eyes don't glaze over today.
(By the way, do *you* know Nelly from R. Kelly?)

Oh, Mustangs! Oh, Monkees!
Oh, when did *USA Today*
get more interesting than *Tiger Beat*?
We're *not* middle-aged. We *can't* be.
Middle-aged is our parents.
Middle-aged is "Where are the Rolaids?"
Middle-aged is Lawrence Welk.
Or was, before Boomers.

Now middle-aged is digital cameras
and SUVs and Oprah,
e-Bay, WiFi, and
Home and Garden TV.
Is it more traumatic for us because our milestone
came at the millenium?

More frightening because the images
of "2001: Space Odyssey" and "In the Year 2525"
grow more realistic every day?
More depressing because, in spite of
all the collagen and Clairol
and Nordic Traks and Nutrasweet
and Viagra and Vitamin E,
we still can't party all night
and perform the next day like we used to?

We're healthier, hipper and,
because life expectancies continue to grow,
we aren't *really* middle-aged,
but we *are* still forty.
Strike up the band?

Laughter

The Domestic Goddess Blues

I am bored and uninspired,
and I'm reallyreallyreally tired
of cleaning messes I don't make,
that multiply if I take a break!
I'm tired of marquees with grammatical errors,
second-hand smoke and rude slogan wearers,
grocery clerks who act like jerks,
and potholes that ruin my tires.

I'm pondering revolt: I'll sit at home,
sip champagne all day, leave Lifetime on,
ignore the laundry, implode the oven,
nap if I want to, or maybe do nothing!
I don't see me dusting or vacuuming soon
and if you should find that inopportune,
if you'd prefer to have things as they were,
too bad.

Taking someone for granted is awfully rude;
That's how women end up in this mood.
It's all in your hands; if you clean up your act,
you can head off this meltdown, and that is a fact!
For a mom who gets help and occasional praise
will bend over backwards and spend all her days
showing her love, beyond and above
any level you might have imagined.

So here's your last chance to quell this rebellion:
act like an angel instead of a hellion
and pick up your towels and socks off the floor,
then perhaps I'll stop screaming and unlock my door.
And perhaps if we go out for dinner tonight,
everything will turn out all right.
(Remember: a mess could induce great distress;
watch yourself, or we're back at square one!)

TLC, Not MTV

I've taken to picking up young boys—
sleepy-eyed ones,
whose dirty-nailed fingers leave sticky,
sugar-cinnamon whorls
on the soft, grey skin of my car seat;
whose laces are
always
untied and
usually
frayed, whose noses need
a good wipe and whose hair
wants brushing—badly.
I ask them about their mothers,
about the math test just past,
the science fair ahead.
We banter a bit about baseball,
or soccer,
or whatever it is that's in season.
Then I move in for the kill.

"So tell me, have you ever kissed a girl?"
Eyes gaping, jaw unhinged,
they sling their heads my way
in revolted disbelief.
"Gah-*ross*!" they yelp,
recoiling at the very thought.
Undeterred and committed to saving
even one still-salvageable soul,
I place a nondescript DVD in their fidgeting hands
then whisper huskily, "Watch and learn!"
Days later,
we cross paths again.
I wave.
"That was disgusting!" they accuse,
thrusting the thing my way.
I smile, confident in knowing
that, come some not-too-far-distant day,
they'll be grateful to Cary Grant, Grace Kelly,
and me.

Swan Song

They want to change my size,
firm my bosom, trim my thighs.
They want to suck my cellulite,
make my stomach flat and tight,
lift my fanny, tuck my chin,
carve me up to make me thin.
I say "Rubbish!" to all that!
Where's the crime in being fat?
Venus wore her width quite well;
it is long past time to quell the

vain designers, diet quacks,
starving models, all those hacks who
make a living out of leaving
bad impressions in the mind of
every woman, smart or dumb,
who sports an ample-sized behind.
Let's hear cheers for Queen Latifah, Emme,
Kathy Bates and Tyne:
here's to bounteous beauties everywhere—
real women—lookin' fine!

Truth and Consequences

So tell me:
if you knew that when
I get home tonight,
these contact-azure eyes will become
plain hazel,
this tousled mane of blonde curls
will come off, leaving wash-and-wear
brown behind,
this sexy silk suit
and these platform power pumps
will give way to flip-flops
and a flannel gown,
would you still
want my number?

Alien Invasion

My friend is drowning in diapers,
in drool and toys and tears.
She is mired on the dark side of Maternia —
that lonely place where mothers are held hostage
while their young temporarily rule the universe.
It's a struggle to breath, to function, to stay sane,
she sobs,
and I remember. I was once there myself.
Should I tell her the truth?
That twelve will make two look like Paradise?
That teen angst makes toddler tantrums look tame?
I think not.
Sometimes, when the truth is out there,
you don't want it to find your address.
And, sometimes, chocolate
is a better gift to give
than honesty.

The Perfect Woman

Katharine Hepburn's spunk,
Ginger Rogers' grace,
Loretta Young's sophistication,
Joanne Woodward's face.

Mother Theresa's devotion,
Florence Nightingale's tenacity,
Rosa Parks' quiet courage,
Sojourner Truth's veracity.

Louisa May Alcott's passion,
Erma Bombeck's wit,
Jane Austen's love of romance,
Jamaica Kincaid's grit.

Helen Keller's determination,
Joan of Arc's integrity,
Jane Goodall's perseverance,
What a woman that would be!

Ode to a Tea Bag

It is the bleakest of mornings
as I crawl from my bed,
red-eyed, rumpled, and decidedly unrefreshed.
My right hip seems not to be working,
my left shoulder has a kink,
already a sinus headache is brewing
and..oh, Lord!..look at my hair!
Limping, snuffling, creaking, moaning,
I make my way toward the kitchen...
grope about in the dark for the kettle,
grope about in the dark for the tea tin,
turn on the stove, feel my spirits rise up
as I reach for a cup in needy anticipation.
Thank you, God, for the glorious gift of Earl Grey.

Ode to Friday

O perfect day!
O glorious day!
O day that dawns so fair!
O blessed day at end of which
One can let down one's hair.

O Friday you are fabulous,
Dear Friday, you're my favorite.
The day that leads from work to play—
No wonder that we savor it!

Love

Okeechobee Love Song

Friends for sixty years,
they did everything together
but die.
Giddy, they pose
on the shores of Lake Okeechobee,
fresh from a shopping spree
in Palm Beach.
Voile dresses, white gloves,
and spectator pumps. . .
on their way to the Orange Bowl,
or perhaps a picnic
by the lake.

The men stand beside them
in white spats and straw hats —
handsome, happy,
on top of the world
in a tiny town at the end of the earth.
They wept together,
slept together,
shared sitters and hambones and
heartaches.
Now all are gone and what's left of the love
are the photographs.

Rescue Mission

Now, she pleads.
and so we go,
tossing toothbrushes in a bag
and commitments out a window
as we escape
en route to healing.
Destination doesn't matter;
it's the intervention that counts.
We've gathered in
posh places and plain—
sprawled out, huddled up.
What matters is the loyalty.

What matters is the love.
What matters is the
indefatigable bungee-cord of caring
that yanks us back from the brink of
whatever
time after time after time.
One can get through anything
with friends.

Bound by Blood

Like Frost's poem, we two diverged
when childhood's happy aura
faded into the dark forest of fertility —
but in inverse directions.
She, of a patent leather and
sensible pumps persuasion,
left Main Street to see the world
on the arm of a dashing commander.
I, a gypsy of midnight with penchants for accents
and adventures du jour,
stayed down South raising rowdy boys
and billy goats.
Our paths meld from time to time.
More often,
we indulge in adagio duets played with gusto
in the key of fiber optics.

Her with news of international analysis,
curried crab bisque, and taffeta ball gowns—
me with tales of church picnics,
the novel of the week,
and belly flops in the backyard pool.
Both of us expound serious repartee, nonetheless,
re life's trials and triumphs and trivialities.
For who but sisters can explore—
with abject honesty—
such subjects as original sin,
suede after Easter,
and skin tags?

The Ballad of Damask Rose

Her elegant French-knot roses lost
their splendor long ago;
where soft pink petals once danced demurely
across the tufted silver sateen throne,
now pale, lackluster threads pill
like discolored dandruff on a drab grey suit.
But like a seer with her crystal ball,
I sit—gingerly—and beckon back my yesterdays.
Every party, every pout, every heartache,
every hope, every guest who passed
through the portals of my childhood home
is there, somewhere,
in this chair.

If it were animal, I would shoot it
and put it out of its misery.
If it were human, I would offer up a prayer
for its soul.
But it is a chair
with arms split and broken,
legs frail and worn,
a seat ripped open and sagging
a broken back, jagged and torn.
And so I caress its pitiful frame like
a cherished friend,
wrap it gently, as if binding its wounds,
and leave my life to linger, intact,
in waiting for another day.

Tete a Tete

We meet for lunch, old friends
toasting old times.
But words and wine and years of
gone-but-not-forgotten memories
make the pasta passe,
the breadsticks boring.

Food is of little consequence
when each word gives birth to
a hundred delicious images,
each touch, a gush of sparkling recollections.
How callous of the waiter to rudely intrude
as we sit chewing and reviewing
Old Love.

A Novel Experience

Welcome back to my life—
to the current chapter, that is.
For you have always been a part
of the anthology.
Tucked into the preface,
present in the dedication,
quoted in the bibliography,
and vastly referenced throughout.
But now—
now you are out of the text
and into the texture of my life—
Teasing, touching, tempting,
tormenting me with your
ruthless Southern charm.
Scarlett would have stood no chance
against you.
How can I?

Back in the Saddle Again

Is this what love is like?
I had forgotten.
The dopey grin I get
when it's you on the phone,
dopier giggles I can't control,
the imploding in my loins
like a one-two punch —
my breath gone, sucked
completely out of my chest.
Ah, yes. My chest.
Tense with the weight of — what?
Joy? Apprehension? Amazement? Lust?
My body spirals, eager and taut,
at the thought of your touch,
of your taste, of your face next to mine.
I like this feeling of being newborn again,
weak-kneed and out of control.
How sad it's a feeling we both know won't last.
(But how wondrous to know it at all!)

Tilt-A-Whirl

Welcome to this new place,
this dimension undiscovered,
this vista unexplored.
I am limp
with desire.
Breathless
at the thought of you
in my arms
in my bed
in my life
in this way.
When you said
yes,
my world went spinning
and glory! what a ride!
Another ticket, please—no, wait!
What I want
is a lifetime pass.

Passion on Ice

Churning in my stomach
burning in my breast
is a hormone-suffused cacophony
that is not at all
ladylike.
I drift, a zombie
in endorphin-drugged stupor,
to the bathroom,
hallway,
kitchen—
aha!
Sticking in my head
amid Hot Pockets and Haagen-Daaz,
I gulp gusts of swirling frosted air
and sigh.
Ye gods!
Was love ever like this before?

Connoisseur

Though my life is rife with complexities,
my heart celebrates simple joys:
a forsythia's first fragile bloom,
the sun's rays splayed through a stand of pines,
Vivaldi and Merlot on a May afternoon,
sleeping babies—any species at all.
And you, my love,
with your no-frills approach to life—
your keep-it-simple,
cut-to-the-chase,
bottom-line-kind of mind.
You are exquisite vanilla
in my too-many flavored world.

Loss

Drive-By Picture Show

Wailing soundlessly,
what the old ones would have called
keening,
what the new breed calls
a photo op,
she sways and clutches, croons
and convulses—
the washed-to-death, faded
red gauze of her dollar-store housedress
brightened by the brilliant red
of her baby boy's life force.

OhGodohGodohnoohnoooooooo
It could be a scene from CSI,
or the latest from Tarentino,
but it is Truth.
Bigger than any screen's expanse,
harsher than any critic,
and the actors only get one take,
because in Life,
there are no stand-ins.

Last Laugh

I am mowing the lawn at your house,
sweating in the late spring sun,
breathing hard—okay, panting—
when I hear you laugh.
It is the laugh I loved best: full
and throaty; musical, with whoops—
the kind they say adds years to life,
except yours is over.

For five months I have missed you,
have wept over popcorn in the grocery aisle,
pink pumps at Penney's, hymns at church,
a blaze of azaleas in a neighbor's yard—
things you would have loved, did love.
It is in these imperceptible places, these
minor moments of my life where you used to be
and now aren't, that I miss you most.

But here is your laugh,
come back to mock my middle-aged,
out of shape self as I slump, spent,
against your Japanese maple.
Hilarious indeed that while I am about the
yardwork you adored and I abhore,
you check in with a laugh to give me
a second wind.

Coming to Terms

It is but a part of my whole.
Ravaged. Rotted. Rendered unacceptable
by the powers that be.
Off with it!
Out with it!
I cast thee aside!
Begone from my broccoli-laced,
anti-oxidized body —
My fat-free, smoke-free,
Cabernet-every day worthless self!
You traitor!
You turncoat!
You cheating, backstabbing blob of
selfish cells!
How dare you upend my world!
How dare you leave me like this!
Facing death.
Facing life.
Facing you.

Retrospect

You ripped me—
effortlessly—
like a kid tearing cellophane
from a jelly roll.
How dare you! I *matter*!
And you've no right to
blaspheme my mind
spit on my pride
laugh at my dreams
and move on.
But you did,
and the only satisfaction
you've left open to me
is to hate you
on paper.

Windowseat

From my window I see
two handsome horses standing,
clove coats glistening
in the warm spring sunlight.
Circling the violet-sprigged pasture,
they share whinnies and inherent awareness
that this pine-fragrant paradise
is a place they're happy to be.

From your window you see
two handsome men standing,
white coats billowing
in the cool spring breeze.
Crossing the dementia-dotted courtyard,
they share whispers and avowed affirmations
that this pine-scented purgatory
is a place they'd hate to be.

Clickety-Clack,
Please Carry Me Back

Like Susannah,
she came from Alabama.
No banjo on her knee,
just a collie named Ring as, swiftly,
the train left cotton fields back home
for strawberry fields in the Sunshine State.
It would be warmer, Papa said,
and the orange trees are so green!
But Papa died and it was hot,
so very, very hot.
Even Ring grew to
hate the sultry-sweet
smell of citrus.

The First Christmas

Uncertain,
she stands cross-armed,
the big box of all that was Christmas—
for fifty-six years, seven months
and five days—
before her.
Lips pursing, then stretching taut,
pursing,and stretching taut,
she inhales
then sits
and slowly unlaps the worn pasteboard flaps
he interlocked
last New Year's Day.
How can it be Christmas?
How can there be carols
and tinsel and joy
when her heart is an empty tomb?

Wet, her shadowed eyes catch sight
of a tiny black velvet boot.
Unbidden, a smile
plays across her rigid mouth.
Memories come of the many branches
from which Kris Kringle's diminutive boot
has dangled,
of the many chubby, sticky hands
whose grasps have crushed its nap.
Stirred, yet still subdued,
her fingers follow another sighting,
to a knobby stone, glue-studded
and smudged with dirt.
Garnished with raveled gold
rick-rack,
the little rock lights her heart
and spawns a grin.

"It looks like an angel!"
their youngest exclaimed
the summer they'd plucked it
from an icy Carolina stream.
"Does not. It's a ghost!"
"You're crazy. It's a bird!"
And thus the argument ensued.
By Christmas, the only point on which
they had agreed was that
the little rock belonged upon the tree—
a recurring testament
to that good time had by all.
The rock found a place of honor every year—
its form perennially debated,
its legacy now priceless.

Instinctively,
her time-mottled, trembling hand engulfs it,
embraces all that lies within this mummied cache —
not just the beat-up, bucktoothed pine cones,
squashed, shredded cotton puff snowmen,
sagging, threadbare stockings,
peeling, bulbous lights —
but the images
and indulgences
and affinities
and affection
laced through every layer.
Inhaling again,
with purpose this time,
she grabs one flap of the box on either end
and drags its unwieldy mass into the den.

It *can* be Christmas, she concedes.
Not the same Christmas,
not *their* Christmas,
but Christmas nonetheless.
Like the little rock,
his legacy would linger,
the memories
dangling in her heart
like cherished heirlooms.

Alternative Lifestyle

Like a mainsail whipped 'round
by a renegade windshear,
she teeters clumsily,
stepping onto the dawn-bridge to
life alone.
Not distraught, exactly.
nor paralyzed or afraid,
but perplexed, perhaps.
Caught off guard and unprepared
to so abruptly implement
Plan B.
They were going to grow old together,
but, suddenly, one is gone
and the other is alone.
It wasn't at all what they'd
cautiously, carefully
planned.

Lessons

Uteropian Myth

We cannot do it all;
It was a lie.
One can only be subdivided
A finite number of times;
1440 minutes can only expand
to encompass so much.
Oh, we can *taste* it all —
snitch a handful of corporate accomplishment…
a quick nibble of connubial bliss…
and then, mouths still full,
we stuff in a morsel of motherhood…
a tidbit of time to ourselves.

But this is no sumptuous banquet:
this picked-over buffet of budget canapés
and fast food hors d'oeuvres
leaves us all still hungry.
Still, in those rare, rare moments
when we manage to steal away and gorge
to our heart's content,
the sating is glorious.

Parameter

She is a gentle woman—pretty,
with a sweet smile that is honest and warm.
We would be friends if we had the time
but we don't and so we are
barely more than acquaintances—
except that she comforts my mother
when I am not there,
soothes her in the night,
wipes the oatmeal from her chin.
And because even though
she has to do those things—it is her job—
she does not have to do them
with love, and so I love her.

I do not know her favorite color
or her childhood heroes,
but I know she adores her children,
enjoys her job, and loves to laugh.
She is a loyal friend, busy mother,
with a beautiful son and compassionate heart.
I think of us as alike until she tells me a story one day
and I am aware that no matter how many tears
I might shed for her pain, I can't *know* her pain;
no one will ever call my child "nigger."

Volley

This woman
with her sleek skull cap
of crisp silver curls,
tennis-taut thighs,
who plays bridge
with "the girls."
This woman
who has sandwiched in
church
and community,
and the barest whisper of a career,
between raising Perfect Children
and being the Perfect Wife.
This woman,
if she had it all to do over again,
might do it
differently.

Perspective Is Everything

I

I'm going now, she announces,
to an old ladies' home.
I've loved my house, but it's too empty.
I've loved my life, but it's too long.
I've loved my mind, but it is going.
I've loved my man, but he is gone.
I am too old for parties, for picnics, for plays. . .
even strolls in the park, I think.
I will just settle in, write a few letters,
crochet a few stitches,
and die.

II

Who says I'm old?
I can run rings around you Boomers—
wipe the floor with you cocky Gen-X, Y, and Zs!
Grandma Moses was just getting started at my age,
and Clara Barton, and Colonel Sanders. . .
so don't talk to *me* about about the brilliance of youth.
I can't walk anymore. Big deal!
Can't see, can't hear. . .annoying, but
hardly fatal.
Give me my computer and get out of my way;
I've got a chat date to visit the Louvre.

Existence 101

Here's what I think:
God put us here to do more than take up space
and mow grass.
We are here to contribute something.
Teachers, doctors, scientists, artists—all shoo-ins.
Pro ballplayers, fashion designers—on shaky ground.
Most of us fall somewhere in between.
Yesterday, for example, I made my family's favorite
dessert, smiled at a solemn old man, and let three
strangers go ahead of me in the turn lane.
Today, however, I fear I owe the universe
a sizable debt
for the peace, love, and joy my black mood
sucked straight out of the ozone.
So be it.
We are not perfect, and there is no grade.
There is only opportunity.
Carpe carefully.

Epitaph

At the end,
will it matter that
the mail was always read,
the kitchen always, *always* clean,
that every day I made my bed?
Are there rewards
for noble rituals like
one hundred strokes a night,
flossing after every meal,
and crossing only with the light?
There is dignity in order;
regard for rules *should* remain high.

But good behavior's not the
coup I want to cling to when I die.
I want to recollect crisp morning strolls
and dancing kites,
a llama's long black lashes,
breezy, salt-tinged, shipboard nights.
To cherish through eternity,
a torrid kiss seems apt,
or images of mountains climbed,
or presents gaily wrapped.
I only know that when I go,
I want to take along more memories
than never having set the table wrong!

Upon Reflection

God, if we get a Round Two,
there are things I would not do
again:
I would not work in retail.
I would not spend Thanksgiving alone.
I would definitely not go out with
that creep from the Chrysler place.

There are things I would do differently:
I would paint rooms turquoise
and fuschia and lime
instead of beige.
I would spend more money on massages
instead of on late fees.
I would buy stock in Amazon
instead of Enron.

I would go caroling
and take long walks in the wood
more often, eat
fresh raspberries and ripe pineapple
every day,
spend more time on a porch,
less time in a car,
and revel
in the glorious wisdom that comes
with age.

Testament

When I am an old woman,
I shall not wear purple with a red hat;
I shall not wear anything at all!
I shall join a nudist colony in the south of France
and stun eighty years worth of kinfolk and friends
with my broad-minded acceptance of my
beautiful, broad-beamed self and my amazing
recovery from a lifetime of latex dependency.

Or
I shall follow the example of Miss Lillian and
perambulate with the Peace Corps into the wilds
of some uncertain, uncivilized country
where my octogenarian expertise
with words and wood and mascara wands
will imbue untold numbers of tribal women
with the gifts of literature, lovely log houses,
and longer lashes.

Or
I shall purchase a pavillion near Walden Pond
and open a restaurant for starving artistes.
The walls will be covered with
register tape sonnets and paper napkin sketches
and I'll serve chai and bagels and grits
and play beach music and Bach
until dawn.

But
whatever I do in my final days,
I shall not wear purple with a red hat,
and I shall not go gentle into
that last good night.

About the Author

Jayne Jaudon Ferrer lives in Greenville, SC. A former advertising copywriter, she speaks frequently about creative writing, poetry appreciation, and coping with Alzheimer's Disease. Please visit her website at www.jaynejaudonferrer.com for more information.